Marcus Pfister

Aaron's Secret Message

Copyright © 2005 by C. Bertelsmann Jugendbuch Verlag, a division of Verlagsgruppe Random House GmbH, Munich
First published in Germany under the title *Ein Glücksstern für Lukas*.
English translation copyright © 2005 by North-South Books Inc., New York

All rights reserved. No part of this book may be reproduced or utilized in any form or by any means, electronic
or mechanical, including photocopying, recording, or any information storage and retrieval system,
without permission in writing from the publisher.

First published in the United States, Great Britain,
Canada, Australia, and New Zealand in 2005 by North-South Books,
an imprint of NordSüd Verlag AG, Gossau Zürich, Switzerland.
Distributed in the United States by North-South Books Inc., New York.

Library of Congress Cataloging-in-Publication Data is available.
A CIP catalogue record for this book is available from The British Library.
ISBN 0-7358-2020-1 (trade edition)
1 3 5 7 9 10 8 6 4 2
ISBN 0-7358-2021-X (library edition)
1 3 5 7 9 10 8 6 4 2
Printed in Belgium

Marcus Pfister

Aaron's Secret Message

Translated by Marianne Martens

NORTH-SOUTH BOOKS / NEW YORK / LONDON

Aaron looked through the open window at the clear night sky over Bethlehem. He loved to look at the stars before he went to sleep. For the past few days, he'd been paying special attention to one particular star. It seemed to grow brighter each night—and bigger, too. Perhaps it's my special star, thought Aaron as he closed the window. And with that wonderful thought, he fell asleep.

His special star stayed with him as he slept. In his dreams the star grew larger and larger and came closer and closer until it was shining down right over his bed. It seemed to be calling to Aaron with a secret message. Aaron got up and followed the star out of the house and across a field. The night was crystal clear, but bitterly cold. Barefoot and still wearing his nightshirt, Aaron hurried after the star. It led him to a stable that looked somehow familiar.

Suddenly, Aaron woke. His feet were freezing. The blanket had fallen off the bed. Quickly he tucked it back in place, snuggled down, and fell asleep.

By the next morning, he'd forgotten the dream. So much was happening in the little town of Bethlehem! After breakfast, Aaron ran out into the narrow streets, to join in the excitement. People were arriving from all around to be counted in the census, as Caesar Augustus had commanded.

Just that morning, two families had asked to stay in Aaron's house, and Aaron's father had made them comfortable in the two guest rooms.

Aaron was caught up in the noise and confusion of the bustling marketplace. The streets were crowded with people, and the merchants competed to sell their goods, one shouting louder than the next.

Aaron noticed a sweet little donkey, drinking greedily at the town fountain. Aaron squeezed through the crowd so that he could touch the donkey's soft coat.

As he was petting it, he heard a voice: "He loves it when you scratch his neck," said a woman. She sat on a stone wall nearby. It was clear from her large belly that she was going to have a baby. She looked very tired.

Soon her husband appeared and spoke briefly to her. He helped her onto the donkey, then they moved off, disappearing into the crowd.

All afternoon more people arrived at Aaron's front door, looking for a place to stay. Toward evening, Aaron heard familiar voices. Curious, he crept to the door, and there were the man and woman he'd seen at the fountain that morning.

His father told them that he was sorry, but they had no more room.

The door had barely closed before Aaron ran to his father. He told him about meeting the couple at the fountain. "Are you *sure* there's no room here?" he asked. "They could sleep in my bed."

"Come now, Aaron," said his father. "We're crowded enough with the two families that are already staying here. I'm sure that couple will find something."

Aaron wasn't sure at all. It was already quite late, and there were
probably hundreds of people still looking for places to stay. Once
again, he left the house and followed the couple with the donkey as
they went from door to door. But there were no rooms left in all of
Bethlehem.

Tired and dismayed, the man and his wife sat to rest on a stone wall.

Aaron raced back home.

"Father," he said urgently. "We have to do something about that couple!"

"No, Aaron. I told you before that we already have enough people here. Our house is completely full. Why, we don't even have a place for the donkey."

"A place for the donkey?" Aaron's eyes opened wide. The secret message! he thought. The dream about the stable!

"But we *do* have a stable! The little hut out there in the field!"

"You're right, Aaron. How could I have forgotten? If it were cleaned up, I'm sure they would be glad to spend the night there. Quick! Lead them to the stable!"

Aaron ran the whole way back to the stone wall where he'd last seen the couple with their donkey.

But no one was there. Had they found a place after all?

Then he saw the little donkey at the end of a narrow street.

The poor woman was crying. Aaron felt a big lump in his throat. Uncertainly, he approached the couple. "I know you're looking for somewhere to stay. I have talked to my parents. Come with me, we can help you!"

Hope flashed across the man's face. Gratefully, he pressed Aaron's hand. "My name is Joseph, and this is my wife, Mary. You've already met the donkey," he said, smiling.

Joseph helped Mary up on the donkey's back, scratched the sturdy little animal's neck affectionately, and followed Aaron through the town.

Soon they arrived at the stable. But what was this? Aaron could hardly believe his eyes. The shabby hut was glowing cheerily, bathed in the light of a beautiful star right overhead. It was Aaron's special star!

There was lots to do. With Joseph helping, Aaron cleared the stable. He put out fresh straw, wood, and water. He ran back and forth and didn't stop until the stable was snug and warm.

"Now we just need blankets!" said Aaron. "I'll run home quickly and get some."

"Take the donkey," said Joseph. "He can carry them for you."

When Aaron returned, bringing blankets, food, and warm tea, he saw Mary sitting on the floor of the stable, holding a tiny bundle in her arms.

"Come here," whispered Mary, reaching out to Aaron. Hesitantly, Aaron stepped closer. He stood openmouthed in wonder. Then, with eyes shining, he carefully laid a blanket over the newborn Child.